GROUNDHOG WEATHER SCHOOL

illustrated by

JOAN HOLUB   **KRISTIN SORRA**

G. P. Putnam's Sons

Penguin Young Readers Group

WEST HARTFORD · PUBLIC LIBRARY

9368

P9-CSH-991

G. P. PUTNAM'S SONS

A division of Penguin Young Readers Group.

Published by The Penguin Group.

Penguin Group (USA) Inc., 375 Hudson Street, New York, NY 10014, U.S.A.

Penguin Group (Canada), 90 Eglinton Avenue East, Suite 700, Toronto, Ontario M4P 2Y3, Canada (a division of Pearson Penguin Canada Inc.).

Penguin Books Ltd, 80 Strand, London WC2R 0RL, England.

Penguin Ireland, 25 St. Stephen's Green, Dublin 2, Ireland (a division of Penguin Books Ltd.).

Penguin Group (Australia), 250 Camberwell Road, Camberwell, Victoria 3124, Australia (a division of Pearson Australia Group Pty Ltd).

Penguin Books India Pvt Ltd, 11 Community Centre, Panchsheel Park, New Delhi - 110 017, India.

Penguin Group (NZ), 67 Apollo Drive, Rosedale, North Shore 0632, New Zealand (a division of Pearson New Zealand Ltd).

Penguin Books (South Africa) (Pty) Ltd, 24 Sturdee Avenue, Rosebank, Johannesburg 2196, South Africa.

Penguin Books Ltd, Registered Offices: 80 Strand, London WC2R 0RL, England.

Text copyright © 2009 by Joan Holub. Illustrations copyright © 2009 by Kristin Sorra.

All rights reserved. This book, or parts thereof, may not be reproduced in any form without permission in writing from the publisher,

G. P. Putnam's Sons, a division of Penguin Young Readers Group, 345 Hudson Street, New York, NY 10014.

G. P. Putnam's Sons, Reg. U.S. Pat. & Tm. Off. The scanning, uploading and distribution of this book via the Internet or via any other means without

the permission of the publisher is illegal and punishable by law. Please purchase only authorized electronic editions, and do not participate in or

encourage electronic piracy of copyrighted materials. Your support of the author's rights is appreciated. The publisher does not have any control over

and does not assume any responsibility for author or third-party websites or their content. Published simultaneously in Canada.

Manufactured in China by South China Printing Co. Ltd. Design by Katrina Damkoehler. Text set in Burghley Medium.

The artist used hand-painted textures of oil on paper, found objects and papers,

all combined and rendered in Photoshop to create the illustrations for this book.

Library of Congress Cataloging-in-Publication Data

Holub, Joan.

Groundhog weather school / Joan Holub ; illustrations by Kristin Sorra.   p. cm.

Summary: When Groundhog realizes he needs helpers all over the country to accurately forecast the weather,

he establishes a school to teach young groundhogs how to properly determine when spring will arrive.

[1. Woodchuck—Fiction. 2. Groundhog Day—Fiction. 3. Spring—Fiction. 4. Schools—Fiction.] I. Sorra, Kristin, ill. II. Title.

PZ7.H7427Gr 2009   [E]—dc22   2008045898

ISBN 978-0-399-24659-3

1 3 5 7 9 10 8 6 4 2

JJ
HOLUB weather
JOAN
J 2/10

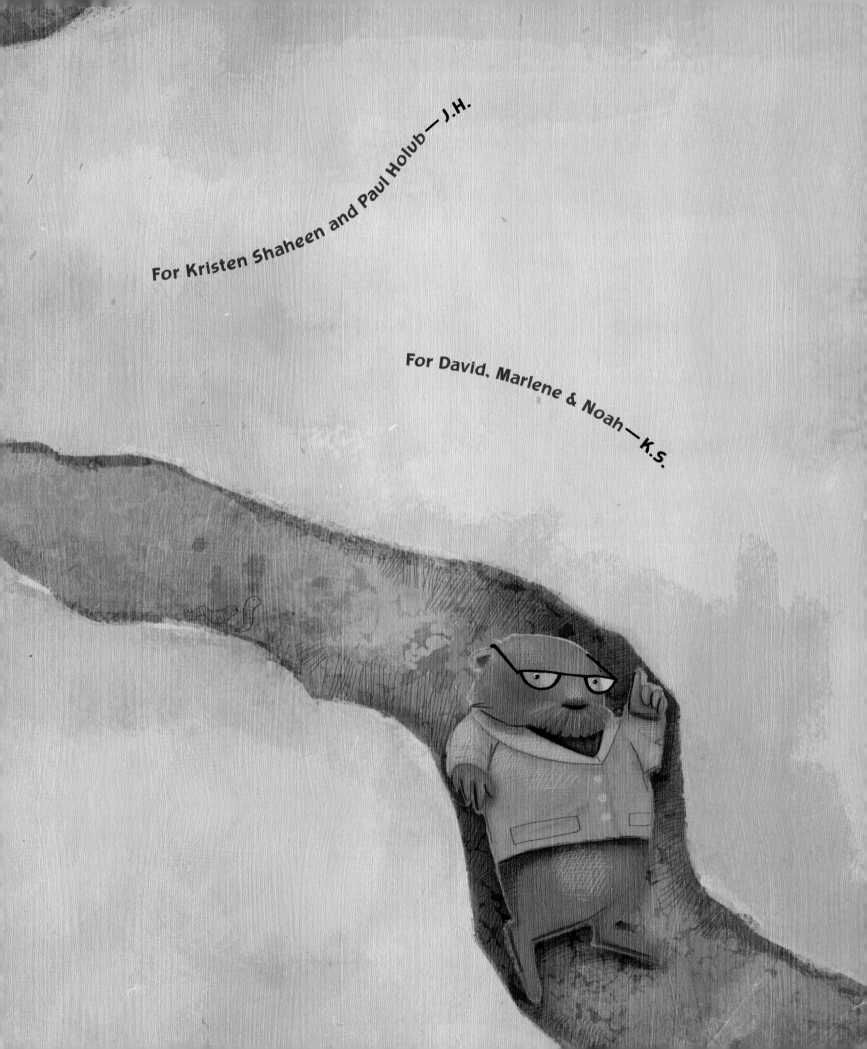

For Kristen Shaheen and Paul Holub—J.H.

For David, Marlene & Noah—K.S.

FEBRUARY
2
Happy Groundhog Day, everyone! I do not see my shadow. That means spring is here.
Groundhog Day Forecast Weather Groundhog Reporting
HOG TV
YAHOO!

R

Dear Weather Groundhog,
You were wrong.
Spring is not here yet.
Maybe you are too far away
to predict the weather
everywhere. Could you get
more groundhogs to help you
next year?

Signed,
Rabbit

bbit
rrow #2
w York,

DEA

Groundhog,

a mistake.

still winter.

Signed,
Monkey

ther groundhog
ong. It is not
pring today.

Signed,
PIG

Hmm. Rabbit's right—I do need some help. But how will I find enough other groundhogs to help me predict the weather all over North America?

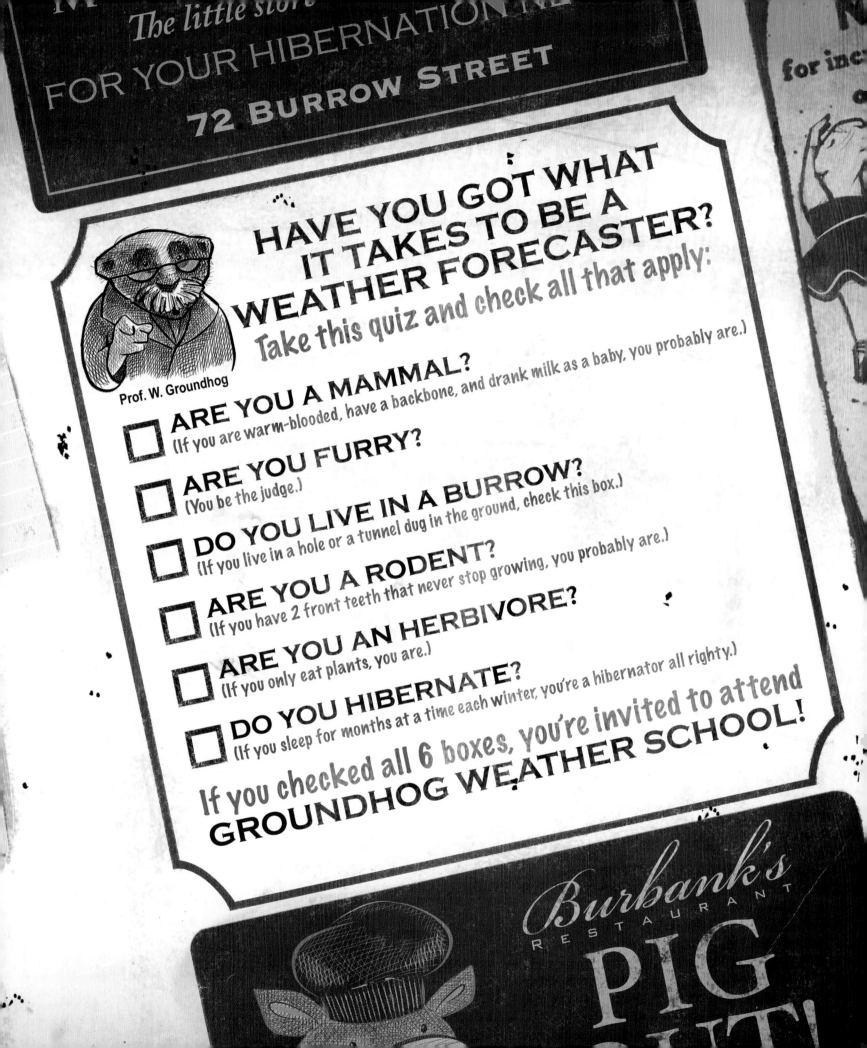

Welcome to your first day at Groundhog Weather School, class. Let's begin by saying the pledge.

PLEDGE of HOG-ALLEGIANCE

We, the students of
Groundhog Weather School,
pledge to come out of our burrows
on February second
to look for our shadows,
and to remember that
if we don't see our shadows,
it means spring is here;
if we do see our shadows,
it means there'll be
six more weeks of winter.

GEHOGRAPHY

COYOTE

Class, please tell us about yourselves.

We watch out for these predators. My eyes, ears, and nose are good danger detectors. If a predator is near, I run for my burrow. I can't run fast, only about ten miles per hour.

We're the only animals with a holiday named after us.

HAPPY GROUNDHOG DAY!

Aren't you forgetting Turkey Day?

Squirrels, chipmunks, and prairie dogs are our relatives. We're all part of a big rodent family called marmots.

G my name is Groundhog. I'm smaller than a beaver, but bigger than a squirrel. And I weigh ten pounds.

GREAT-UNCLE SQUIRRELY & GREAT-AUNT NUTSY

FOX

DOG

WOLF

BOBCAT

HAWK

OWL

EAGLE

HUMAN

Most of us live in areas that get very cold in winter, like the northeast or central part of the United States and in Canada.

Groundhog Day began here in Pennsylvania.

We dig holes and eat farm crops. So some states don't allow groundhogs— except for graduates of Groundhog Weather School, of course!

Like most groundhogs in the northeastern United States, I prefer to be called a woodchuck. In the Appalachian Mountains, groundhogs are called whistle pigs because we whistle to warn other groundhogs of danger.

RANGE OF GROUNDHOGS IN NORTH AMERICA

Well done, class! Now let's visit the library. Research reports are due on the next page.

FAMOUS ★ FURRY ★ HOGNOSTICATORS

Punxsutawney Phil
Punxsutawney, Pennsylvania
- made his first weather prediction in 1886
- met U.S. President Ronald Reagan
- starred in a movie called Groundhog Day

Wiarton Willie
Wiarton, Ontario, Canada
- a rare white (albino) groundhog with pink eyes
- tries to predict which football team will win the Super Bowl
- gets visitors from as far away as Pakistan

General Beauregard Lee
Lilburn, Georgia
- lives in a small white house at the Yellow River Game Ranch
- has been on the *Today* show and on Animal Planet
- has an honorary college degree

Jimmy the Groundhog
Sun Prairie, Wisconsin

- is visited by as many as 500 people each Groundhog Day
- has a weather hotline
- visits Wisconsin schools

Buckeye Chuck
Marion, Ohio

• the official Ohio state groundhog
• lives in a comfy straw-lined box in a park
• visits a radio station on Groundhog Day to give his weather forecast

Pierre C. Shadeaux
New Iberia, Louisiana
• is really a nutria, a rodent with webbed feet and a long tail that lives in marshland or swamps
• has a Cajun-style house, which is moved to the Bouligny Plaza park each year for a big Groundhog Day celebration

Staten Island Chuck
Staten Island, New York
• has a house with a thermometer in the roof
• lives at the Staten Island Zoo
• ice statues of him are carved on February 2

Sir Walter Wally
Raleigh, North Carolina

• in the week before Ground-hog Day, kids record their weather observations. When the mayor announces Wally's weather forecast at the North Carolina Museum of Natural Sciences, kids watch to see if Wally's prediction turns out to be right

NATURE'S WEATHER PREDICTORS

Some plants and animals can help predict the weather.

A tree's leaves can predict storms. Leaves curl upward so their underside shows if there is moisture in the air and a strong wind is blowing.

ACHOO!

Cows don't like wind blowing in their faces, so they stand with their backsides to the wind. Winds blowing from the west usually bring good weather. So if a cow's tail is turned toward the west, it often means good weather is coming.

Wet honeybees are too heavy to fly. They stay near their hive if rain is coming.

Moo!

If a pinecone's leaves fold inward, it may rain. In dry weather, they fold outward.

Moo to you too.

LUKE HOWARD created a system for classifying and naming different cloud shapes. It includes cumulus, cirrus, and stratus clouds.

WILSON "SNOWFLAKE" BENTLEY was a farmer in Vermont who took thousands of pictures of individual snowflakes. This helped scientists understand how snowflakes form.

WEATHER MEN

BAROMETER

Impressive.

EVANGELISTA TORRICELLI invented the barometer, which measures air pressure. If air is not pressing hard against the earth, it's called a low-pressure system. That often means it will rain. Can you guess what a high-pressure system means?

PROFESSOR THEODORE FUJITA was nicknamed "Mr. Tornado" because he helped figure out how to measure the wind speed inside a tornado.

Lunchtime, everyone! Be sure you hog out. It's important to add as much fat to our bodies as we can before hibernation begins.

TODAY'S LUNCH MENU
ALFALFA SALAD
CARROT SOUP
SCALLION SOUP
FRUIT CUP
FRESH FRUIT
VEGETARIAN PLATE
CLOVER SURPRISE
CUP OF SEEDS

Why do we have to hibernate in the winter?

Yeah! I'm not sleepy.

We hibernate for four or five months between October and March because it's cold and food is hard to find.

During hibernation we are in a deep sleep. Our heartbeats slow down, our body temperatures drop, and we only breathe about once every four minutes! We don't need to eat because we live off of the fat our bodies have stored. So eat up, groundhogs!

My friend Frog hibernates at the bottom of a stream where the water doesn't freeze.

My friend Bat hibernates in a cave, with her wings tucked close to keep her warm.

HOW TO BUILD A BURROW

1. Dig a hole in the ground to make your front door.

2. Keep digging. Chomp through any roots. This will help wear down your claws and teeth so they don't grow too long.

3. We can dig about five feet in one day. If you want a simple burrow, dig about fifteen feet of tunnel. If you want a fancy one, dig up to forty feet.

4. Make a few rooms along the way, such as a bedroom, a bathroom, and a storeroom for snacks.

5. Be sure to make a back door in case you need to make a quick escape!

BURROW SWEET BURROW

DON'T FORGET TO FLUSH!

THE REASONS

We have a surprise for you, Professor— a skit about seasons.

In North America, a year is divided into four seasons of three months each. The seasons are winter, spring, summer, and fall.

I'm winter. I begin around December 21 at the winter solstice, which is the shortest day of the year.

I'm spring. I begin around March 21 at the spring equinox, when day and night are the same length.

I'm summer. I begin around June 21 at the summer solstice, which is the longest day of the year.

for SEASONS
I'm fall. I begin around September 21 at the fall equinox, when day and night are the same length.
There are two reasons why we have seasons: 1. Planet Earth orbits (goes around) the sun. 2. The Earth is tilted.
The equator is an imaginary line that divides Earth into two halves called hemispheres. When a hemisphere tilts toward the sun, it's warmer, as in summer. When it tilts away, it's colder, as in winter.
Wonderful. I'm so proud of you!

Move far from the light to make a small shadow.
Come close to the light to make a big shadow.
At night there are no shadows because there's no sunlight.
Who's hogging the flashlight?
Excellent! I think *you're* all ready for the final exam.

the BIG test

A MULTIPLE CHOICE QUIZ

Please circle the correct answer:

1. What day do you come out of your burrow?
a. on your birthday
b. on February 2nd
c. on February 32nd

2. What do you look for when you come out?
a. a valentine
b. a shadow
c. a pot of gold

3. If you see it (see answer to number 2), what does it mean?
a. spring is here
b. summer vacation is here
c. six more weeks of winter

4. If you don't see it, what does it mean?
a. you are invisible
b. spring is here
c. six more years of school

5. Whether you see it or not, what's the next thing you do?
a. go back to sleep
b. have a snack
c. report the results to Groundhog Headquarters

That's one BIG test!

(Answers: 1b, 2b, 3c, 4b, 5c)

OCTOBER
Columbus Day

Texas

New York

Florida

California

NOVEMBER
Thanksgiving

Yum!

DECEMBER
Christmas, Hanukkah

For me? I shouldn't have.

JANUARY
Martin Luther King Jr. Day

★ FEB 2nd... ⭐
Wake up! IT'S GROUNDHOG DAY!

It's February 2. At school headquarters, weather reports are coming in from every Groundhog Weather School graduate. Will there be more winter? Or is it time for spring?
Does seeing a shadow in lightning count?
Hello? Groundhog Weather School here.
Sh-sh-sh-shadow!
What's your report?
Achoo! No sdado.
I see a dog. Does that count?

FEBRUARY
2
Happy Groundhog Day, everyone! I had some help this year from the graduates of Groundhog Weather School. Most of us saw our shadows, including me. So it's a sure bet that winter will last for six more weeks!
Groundhog Day Forecast Weather Groundhog Reporting
HOG TV
Professor Groundhog took my advice and got some help. He's sure to be right this time.

How did Groundhog Day get started?

Long ago, farmers in Europe watched for badgers and bears to wake up from hibernation, hoping this indicated that winter had ended. If spring was coming, it would be safe to plant crops without worrying they might freeze. When these farmers settled in Pennsylvania in the 1700s, there were lots of groundhogs around, so the farmers began watching them wake up instead.

But why choose February 2?

Ancient Romans and other past civilizations could hardly wait for warm spring weather to arrive. February 2 comes about halfway between the shortest day of the year (December 21) and the beginning of spring (March 21), so it was a good day to celebrate the coming season. In North America, these February 2 celebrations became Groundhog Day.

Who's better at predicting the weather—a groundhog or you?

Groundhog weather predictions are only right about one third of the time. But it's fun to celebrate Groundhog Day and watch for winter to eventually turn into spring. This February 2, do you hope spring will come right away or do you hope winter lasts longer? Which do you think will happen? Write down your prediction and see if it comes true.

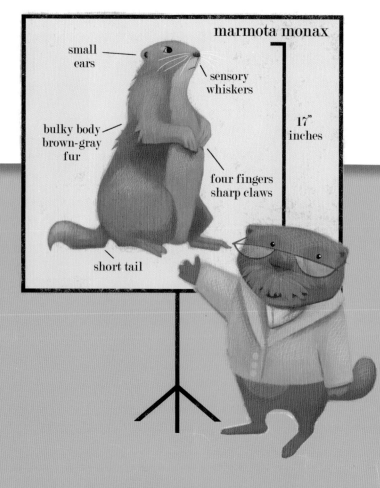

marmota monax

small ears

sensory whiskers

bulky body brown-gray fur

17" inches

four fingers sharp claws

short tail